Anonymous

My Lady's Cabinet

Decorated with Drawings and Miniatures

Anonymous

My Lady's Cabinet
Decorated with Drawings and Miniatures

ISBN/EAN: 9783337117467

Printed in Europe, USA, Canada, Australia, Japan

Cover: Foto ©Andreas Hilbeck / pixelio.de

More available books at **www.hansebooks.com**

MY LADY'S CABINET

DECORATED WITH DRAWINGS

AND MINIATURES

LONDON:

SAMPSON LOW, MARSTON, LOW, AND SEARLE,

CROWN BUILDINGS, FLEET STREET.

1873.

PREFACE.

 VISIT to a lady's boudoir, daintily hung with water-colour drawings and many family portraits in their little oval frames, suggested the plan of decoration adopted in these pages.

Though we are unable to reproduce the landscapes of Turner, Stanfield and Birket Foster, or the charming portraits of Boxall, Frith and Richmond in all their beauty, we can, at least, give faithful copies of them in miniature; and it is hoped that a quarter of an hour spent in looking through our little gallery will somewhat compensate those who are unable to see the original gems of art which are included in "My Lady's Cabinet."

J. C.

BOURNEMOUTH,
November, 1872.

SCENE FROM THE "PILGRIM'S
PROGRESS."

THOMAS STOTHARD, R.A.

TOURS, ON THE LOIRE.

J. M. W. TURNER, R.A.

NOBODY COMING TO MARRY ME.

B. R. FAULKNER.

ITALIAN WATER-CARRIER.

R. EDMONSTONE.

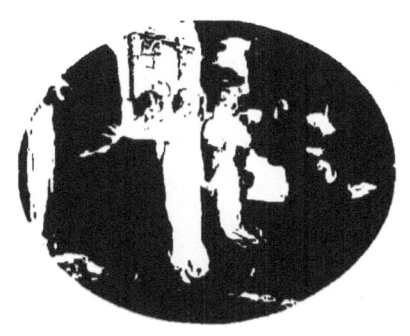

HIGHLAND SHOOTING BOX

FREDERICK TAYLER.

MAY DAY.

C. R. LESLIE, R.A.

LIGHT-TOWERS ON THE HEVE.

J. M. W. TURNER, R.A.

CHATEAU GAILLARD.

J. M. W. TURNER, R.A.

ANCONA, ITALY.

W. BROCKEDON.

THE BANKS OF THE SCHELDT.

VAN WERF.

PONTORSON, NORMANDY

WILLIAM DELAMOTTE.

MOUNTAIN SPRITE.

r. WOOD.

LESBIA.

W. P. FRITH. R. A.

CUPID AND PSYCHE.

R. WESTALL, R. A.

ROUEN, ON THE SEINE.

J. M. W. TURNER, R.A.

NORHAM CASTLE.

BIRKET FOSTER.

A SUMMER SUNSET

THOMAS CRESWICK. R.A.

PONT NEUF, PARIS.

J. M. W. TURNER, R.A.

AN ENGLISH GIRL.

R. BUCKNER.

THE BILLET-DOUX.

G. S. NEWTON, R.A.

THE CASTLE BY THE SEA.

I. CRESWICK, R.A.

NANTES, ON THE LOIRE.

J. M. W. TURNER, R.A.

THE DANCING DOG.

W. DELAMOTTE.

NATURE'S FAVOURITE.

W. BOXALL, R.A.

RICHMOND HILL.

GEORGE BARRETT.

COUNTRY DANCE, "THE TRIUMPH"

THOMAS STOTHARD, R.A.

.

THE AVENUE.

THOMAS CRESWICK, R.A.

AMBOISE, ON THE LOIRE

J. M. W. TURNER, R.A.

HOLY EYES.

As shining beacons solely to light to heaven.

J. G. MIDDLETON.

LEA.

Her hands and eyes were instant li

V. DE VALENTINI

BEAUGENCY ON THE LOIRE.

J. M. W. TURNER, R.A.

THE DESERTED

G. S. NEWTON, R.A.

THE KEY-NOTE.

J. G. MIDDLETON.

THE HARVEST-FIELD.

BIRKET FOSTER.

THE VILLAGE CHURCH

BIRKET FOSTER.

DOLLY VARDEN.

JOHN ABSOLON.

THE MAY QUEEN.

W. BOXALL, R. A.

CAUDEBEC, ON THE SEINE.

J. M. W. TURNER, R. A.

PSYCHE.

SIR W. BEECHEY, K.A.

DOROTHEA.

I. G. MIDDLETON.

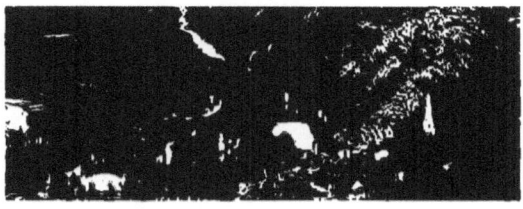

MARGARET RAMSAY.

W. BONALL, R.A.

LALLA ROOKH.

A. DI VALENTINI.

COTEAUX DE MAUVES.

J. M. W. TURNER, R.A.

THE HAWKING PARTY.

A. COOPER, R.A.

A COAST SCENE.

J. HOLLAND.

A SUMMER SUNSET.

BIRKET FOSTER.

OUR HOMESTEAD.

BIRKET FOSTER.

THE PLEASING THOUGHT.

WILLIAM BOXALL, R.A.

THE GLEANER.

SIR EDWIN LANDSEER, R.A.

A GRECIAN MAID

G. S. NEWTON, R.A.

.

THE BLIND PIPER.

LUDWIG RICHTER.

DOMESTIC HAPPINESS.

LUDWIG RICHTER.

TOURS, JUNCTION OF THE LOIRE
AND CHER

J. M. W. TURNER, R. A.

FLORA MAC IVOR.

A. E. CHALON, R. A.

LAUGHING EYES.

W. P. FRITH, R.A

A SURREY LANE.

R. REDGRAVE, R.A

NORA CREINA.

W. P. FRITH, R.A.

THE HUNTSMAN'S HORN.

FREDERICK TAYLER.

AN AUBERGE AT ST. OMER,
FLANDERS.

WILLIAM DELAMOTTE.

THE NOON-DAY MEAL.

THOMAS CRESWICK, R. A.

SUMMER ROSES

TONY JOHANNOT.

A PORTRAIT.

W. BOXALL. R.A.

RIETZ, NEAR SAUMUR.

J. M. W. TURNER. R.A.

SCENE ON THE LOIRE

J. M. W. TURNER, R.A.

VIEW ON THE SEINE.

J. M. W. TURNER, R.A.

VENICE

C. BENTLEY.

SCENE FROM THE "PILGRIM'S
PROGRESS."

THOMAS STOTHARD, R. A.

THE STORM IN HARVEST.

R. WESTALL, R.A.

PRAWN FISHERS.

W. COLLINS, R.A.